088460

B   Bancroft, Catherine
       Felix's hat.

Felix's Hat

by Catherine Bancroft and Hannah Coale Gruenberg

pictures by Hannah Coale Gruenberg

Four Winds Press ❖ New York

Maxwell Macmillan Canada   Toronto   Maxwell Macmillan International   New York   Oxford   Singapore   Sydney

Printed and bound in the United States of America
10 9 8 7 6 5 4 3 2 1

The text of this book is set in Egyptian Light.
The illustrations are rendered in watercolor.
Book design by Christy Hale

Library of Congress Cataloging-in-Publication Data
Bancroft, Catherine.
Felix's hat / by Catherine Bancroft and Hannah Coale Gruenberg ;
illustrated by Hannah Coale Gruenberg.—1st ed.
p.   cm.
Summary: When Felix Frog loses his favorite hat, the rest of the
family tries to make him feel better.
ISBN 0-02-708325-X
[1. Frogs—Fiction.   2. Hats—Fiction.   3. Brothers and sisters—
Fiction.]   I. Gruenberg, Hannah Coale, ill.   II. Title.
PZ7.B2177Fe   1993
[E]—dc20   92-10868

To the memory of my father

—C.B.

To all the people in my life
who are my family,
both blood and otherwise

—H.C.G.

That orange hat of Felix's was always getting lost.

It fell under chairs or tumbled behind the bureau or got stuck under the radiator.

But Felix always found it again,

which was lucky, because he hated going anywhere without it.

One day the whole family was going to the pond.
Philomena brought her glossy magazine. Frank had his flippers.
Freda carried her bucket. Baby Phoebe didn't bring anything,
not even a bathing suit. Felix, of course, wore his hat.

While Daddy was getting the car ready, Felix snapped his
goggles tight around his hat to keep it from blowing off as
they drove.

"Does he have to look like that?" his big sister Philomena asked.

When they got to the pond, Felix took his inner tube and ran straight down to the water.

"Good-bye, Frank and Philomena," he called as he jumped into his tube and went paddling off to the water lilies.

The sun was warm. The clouds were fat and white. Lying on his inner tube, Felix thought he was a Cheerio in a bowl of milk.

He thought about a big spoon coming to get some Cheerios, when…

Thunk! Splash!…

The tube bumped right into a rock, and Felix fell in the water.

First, he was sure he was drowning. Then his feet touched
bottom, and he pushed himself back into the tube.

Felix blew water out of his nose.
Boy, did he get back to the shore fast.

"Good heavens, my little frog, where were you?" Mommy Frog said as she wrapped wet Felix in the big, striped towel. "Mommy, a giant spoon crashed into me!" Felix said.

Freda's mouth fell open. "Gee," she said.

Philomena looked him over. "Where's your hat, Felix?" she said.
"Uh-oh," Frank said.

"My hat!" Felix screamed. "Where's my hat?"
"I saw it when you went in the water," Philomena said.
"I want my hat!"
"Now don't get so upset, Felix," Frank said. "We'll find it."

Frank and Felix and Philomena rowed out in their little boat to look for the hat. Philomena rested while Felix looked under a lily pad. They searched around the rock and in the reeds.

Frank even dove underwater. But no hat.

Philomena looked at Felix. "That was a stinky old hat anyway. I bet a duck took it away and is wearing it now."

On the ride home Felix didn't say a word.
He didn't talk to anybody.
It was dark when they got to the house. Felix walked straight to
the big chair and everybody followed him.

"I will not go to bed without my hat," Felix said.

"Oh, honestly," Philomena said.

"Bathtime," Mommy Frog said.

"And I won't take a bath without my hat."

So Felix sat by himself. His head felt very lonely.

After a while Freda came back in
wearing her pajamas.
"Hat," she said, and gave him her
bear. Felix took the teddy bear and
put it on his head.
It was too furry.

Then Phoebe crawled in with her
bottle in her mouth.
She held out her bottle and
Felix put it on his head.
The bottle was too skinny and tall.

Philomena came in carrying her old
yellow blanket. "A blanket can be
very comforting, Felix," she said.
Felix put the blanket on his head.
It just made everything dark.

Frank did a slide into the big chair.
"You know, I could find my old red
baseball hat," Frank said. "If you
want that. It's probably in the garage."
The others looked hopefully at Felix.
Felix shook his head.
He didn't want it.

Felix was getting sleepy, but he couldn't go to bed. Everybody else was getting sleepy, too.

"Off to bed, all of you," Daddy Frog said. "It's late."

"I can't believe you have to sleep in that hat," Philomena said as she went out.

A tear came to Felix's eye.

"Felix," his mother said. She lifted him onto her lap. "I want to tell you a story.

"See the moon?" She pointed out the window. "Somewhere that moon is shining on your hat. And right now there's probably a little animal lying under your hat, feeling all snug and warm. He's saying, 'Thank you, Felix, for giving me such a nice place to sleep.'"

Felix snuggled against Mommy Frog's shoulder.

"What kind of animal do you see, Felix?"

"A turtle," Felix said, and shut his eyes.

Mommy Frog was putting Felix to bed when Frank tiptoed in.
"I finally found it," he whispered. "Here, buddy, it's my old red
hat that I won at the County Fair. It's not your orange one, but
maybe you can wear it anyway."
He put the red hat on Felix's sleepy head.

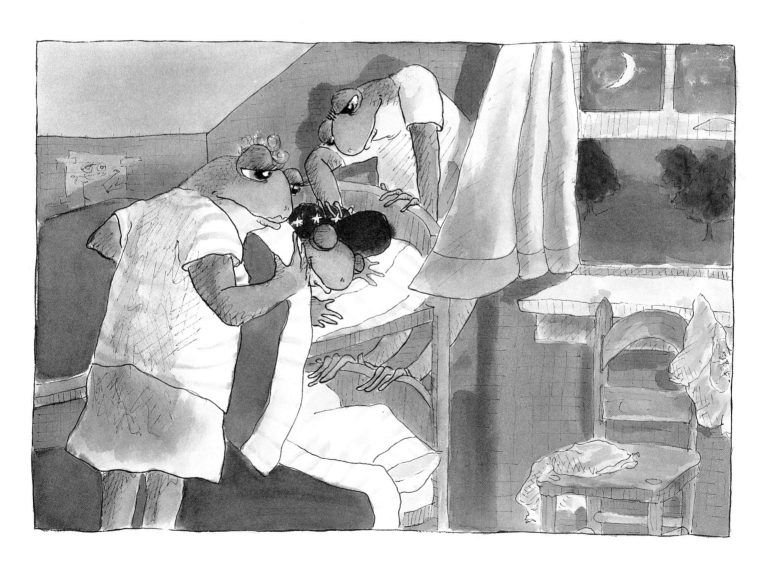

Later that night while Felix was sleeping, he had a dream. In the midnight sky a turtle was flying with Felix's hat in his mouth.

The turtle was coming to return Felix's hat. But when he flew
over Felix's bed and let go of the hat, something strange
happened. As the hat fell it started changing color, so that by
the time it landed on Felix's head, it wasn't orange anymore.
It was red.

When Felix woke up the next morning, his head felt happy. He
jumped out of bed and ran to the bathroom mirror. There was
his new red hat.
"Hey, Frank!" he shouted. "Look!"
Frank came to the bathroom door to see.

"Philomena! Freda! Phoebe!" Felix yelled. "Look what the turtle
brought me!"

"Go back to bed," said Philomena.

"Gaga," said baby Phoebe.

"Breakfast time," called Mommy Frog from the kitchen.

Felix pulled the brim of his hat around to the back, put on his slippers, and trotted happily down to breakfast.

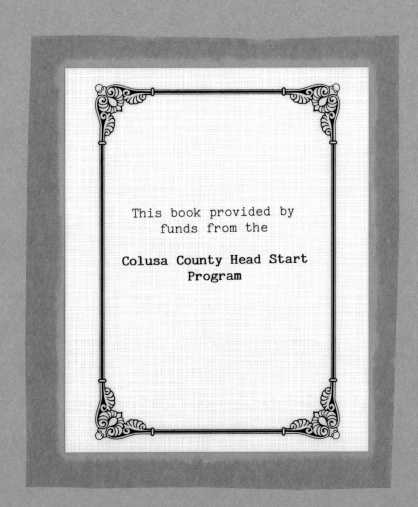